Vroom!

Jill Atkins
Illustrated by Brian Peacock

Rigby

It was spring.
Toad was asleep under a tree.

He opened one big eye.

He opened two big eyes.

"Come on," said Frog. "It's spring.
It's time to go to the pond."

Frog hopped along the path.
Toad crawled along the path.

They came to the road.

Frog looked this way.
Frog looked that way.
"Come on, Toad," said Frog,
and he hopped across the road.

Toad crawled onto the road.

ting-a-ling ting-a-ling

"Look out!" said Frog.
"It's a bicycle!"

The bicycle zoomed down the road.

"That's scary!" said Toad.

"Come on, Toad," said Frog.
Toad crawled on the road.

The car zoomed down the road.

"That's very scary!" said Toad.

Toad crawled on the road.

Toad closed his eyes tight.
"This is the end!" he thought.

A woman got out of the truck.
She picked up Toad.

"Now you can go to the pond," she said.

Toad crawled to the pond.
"Come on, Toad," said Frog.
"It's lovely in here!"